SHASHI AND MAYA
A Life of Courage

Story by Wobine Ishwaran
Illustrations by Kalpart Designs

Order this book online at www.trafford.com
or email orders@trafford.com

Most Trafford titles are also available at major online book retailers.

Note for Librarians: A cataloguing record for this book is available from Library
and Archives Canada at www.collectionscanada.ca/amicus/index-e.html

Printed in Victoria, BC, Canada.

ISBN: 978-1-4269-0184-3 (sc)
ISBN: 978-1-4269-0186-7 (e)

This story is a work of fiction. Names, places and characters are a product
of the author's imagination.

*Our mission is to efficiently provide the world's finest, most comprehensive
book publishing service, enabling every author to experience success.
To find out how to publish your book, your way, and have it available
worldwide, visit us online at www.trafford.com*

Trafford rev. 09/17/2009

 www.trafford.com

North America & international
toll-free: 1 888 232 4444 (USA & Canada)
phone: 250 383 6864 ♦ fax: 812 355 4082

Dedication:

This story is for my friends
and relatives in India

Ask not who they are

They belong to us

They are our Kith and Kin

No matter who they are

Bassavanna
12th century AD
Karnataka, India

Shashi and Maya

One crisp early morning, Shashi decided to go to the fields to help with harvesting. Help was needed to chase away the nasty birds, which swarmed around to pick at the ripe rice kernels.

The children were asked to help by pulling a string with gold and white pieces of paper to scare off the birds. Shashi quickly went to wash his face, put on his shirt and shorts and sandals and set off for his grandfather's rice fields.

Grandfather and his helpers were already busy harvesting the ripe rice stalks, cutting them by hand with a sickle. A large flock of white birds were circling around bothering the workers.

How glad they were when Shashi arrived on the scene!

Soon after, Maya, his younger sister joined them on the farm. The two of them giggled and chatted to their heart's content, while pulling the strings, which were strung across the row of rice plants, to keep the birds at

bay. A little shed on the side of the field protected them from the sun's burning rays. Later on, the children would help to bundle the rice stalks.

The local school was closed for the harvest season and the children were free to help on the farm.

Shashi and Maya lived with their parents; mother Manju, also called Awwa by the kids, father Kollappa or Appa, and Grandfather Adja. Their home was in Shivapuru, a small village in the South of India.

The home was small, but comfortable and well built. There was a stable under the same roof, which housed a cow, a few goats and a bullock. The living area included a veranda, a kitchen, a small prayer room, and a living room that was used as a bedroom at night. The porch in the front of the house was for receiving visitors. On hot nights, the men slept on the porch rolled up in heavy black wool blankets to ward off the mosquitoes.

Work usually ended in the evening with the setting sun. All the workers gathered together and walked home leisurely. Some of the women balanced a bundle of sticks on their heads. Cheerful voices filled the air; here and there a song could be heard.

After washing their hands, feet and faces, Shashi's family entered the cool home where food was ready. Grandfather, his son in law and the young boy, sat down on the clean mats. Mother and Maya served the delicious spicy food.

"Manju, you have cooked another wonderful meal. After all that hard work in the fields, it is such a treat to come home and have this lovely food ready for us," said Grandfather. He always appreciated his daughter's cooking.

"Kollappa, we achieved a lot today. Tomorrow we'll finish and store the harvest. We have a good crop this year. Shashi and Maya were a great help too!" Grandfather added.

Later, when the men in the family had finished eating, Manju and Maya would gather in the kitchen. It was now their turn to enjoy the meal and gossip!

Once everyone had enjoyed the meal and the kitchen was tidied up, bedrolls were spread out on the floor, mosquito nets were hung, and the family got ready to enjoy a good night's sleep.

The Storm

In the morning, dark clouds were drifting in the sky and Grandfather became worried that rain would destroy his crop, so he hurried everyone to the fields.

"Shashi and Maya you come with me to help bundle the rice stalks. We need to bring the harvest in before the rain starts," he said.

The whole family rushed to the field to help with the harvest.

The rice was beautifully ripe and dry

The cut bundles of rice stalks were now ready to be threshed on the ground to loosen the kernels.

And the kernels were collected in large baskets.

At the end of the day Shashi brought the bullock cart, the baskets loaded up and stored in the shed.

Luckily, the harvest was safe just before a fierce storm arrived, with a cloudburst. It rained and rained and didn't stop. The roads in the village started to resemble rivers of muddy water. The howling winds rattled doors and windows. There were lightning flashes across the sky and loud thunder. The cattle in the stable became restless, the goats started to bleat with little whiny voices.

Grandfather looked worried and Mother positioned some buckets and pots under the leaks. The roof was not made to withstand such heavy rainfall. "Awwa, I am scared," whimpered Maya.

"Let's say our evening prayers," suggested her mother.

The family gathered around the oil lamp and started reciting their evening songs of praise.

At last, the rain lessened and the wind quieted down and the family retired to their beds.

Disaster Hits

Heavy rain filled up the large lake- reservoir above the village and suddenly the dam couldn't hold the extra water and burst. An enormous flood thundered down the hill causing mudslides and slowly filling the streets of the village.

Shashi woke up suddenly, he felt his mattress and it was getting wet, and water was rising up all around his bedroll. He jumped up, his feet sloshing through mud and he shouted loudly, "Awwa, Appa, Adja! Wake up there is a flood!"

Then he noticed Maya curled up in her blanket, fast asleep. The water was slowly rising all around her. Quickly he picked her up and ran out of the door. Immediately, they were swept down the hill practically drowning in the muddy flow. The children held on tightly to each other. Maya started to cry, "Awwa, help, Appa help us," but nobody heard them. Miraculously a piece of lumber bumped into them. Shashi grasped it and was able to hoist himself and Maya on top.

Holding on tightly to their precarious raft, they floated away, speeding down the hill, until suddenly, with a big bump, their piece of lumber got stuck against a large tree trunk. There, the scared and chilled children spent a miserable night and most of the next day. The cold waves were rocking the raft to and fro. The chilling winds howled over their heads. Maya and Shashi's little hands were getting stiff with cold. It was almost impossible for Shashi to hold on to his sister, while balancing on the piece of lumber at the same time.

Finally and slowly, the water receded leaving a thick layer of mud behind. The surrounding terraces and the village were in ruin. It was a dreadful sight. There was not a living soul to be seen. There was dead silence. They did not hear a call for help, a cow mowing, or even a dog's bark. A horrid smell filled the air. The frightened boy and girl began to cry again calling out, "Awwa, Appa, Adja. Where are you?" There was no answer to their woeful cries.

The Rescue

Shashi decided they needed to find dry land. He lifted Maya on his back and started wading through the deep mud. It was tough going, he stumbled several times but persevered until at last they came to a road. Exhausted and drenched they collapsed at the roadside. Maya fell asleep with her head on Shashi's lap.

The sun was setting over the desolate environment. Shashi became drowsy. He was hungry, cold, miserable and very tired. He could not keep his eyes open any further and dozed off.

A far off rumbling sound woke them up. "A car is coming Maya," called out Shashi, hoping they would be rescued. A rickety shaking old vehicle rattled along and came to a halt near the children.

"Hey, you two, hop on. I'll drop you off in town near a shelter where you can get food and dry clothes," offered Raju, the driver. A few survivors were already in the van. They moved closer together to make room for the children.

Shashi was hoping to find his parents inside the van, but there were only strangers. They seemed to be survivors from another village. Worriedly, Maya tried to explain to Raju that they had to go and find their parents. The kind man consoled them and said, "Your parents could be in the city already and you might be able to find them at the shelter. Some buses and vans with rescue teams have already picked up survivors of the flood."

"Shashi we might find them in the city," encouraged Maya, who did not want to give up hope.

After a long bumpy ride they arrived in the city. The van dropped everyone off at an emergency rescue shelter. Loving, caring arms embraced the bedraggled children and gave them clean clothes, food and a warm place to sleep.

The Shelter

When Shashi woke up he looked around sleepily and realized that he was not in his home with Appa, Awwa, and Adja. There, amongst women and children he discovered his sister.

Maya was sitting up rubbing her eyes, astounded to find herself in a strange place with a lot of people sitting or lying around on the floor. A kind voice called out, "Come along children, I'll show you the bathroom. Here is a towel for you. Take a bath and then come for breakfast."

Shashi helped Maya bathe. He soaped her back and poured warm water over her head and washed her long tangled hair. They were given dry clothes and Shashi combed Maya's lovely black hair and made a long braid. She almost looked like the lovely girl she was before the disaster. After the bath, all the children sat down to eat in the large dining hall.

Volunteers had cooked rice and dhal and were serving the children first.

Later the men and women were also fed.

"Now we have to go find Awwa, Appa and Adja," said Maya anxiously.

"All right little sister," answered Shashi. "But first we have to look around here in the shelter, they might be here too."

They searched and asked around, but did not find them.

Someone told them that there was one more shelter with survivors not far down the street. Shashi took Maya by the hand and they left the shelter

Lost in the big City

Carefully, they started walking along the side of the busy street, under the huge shady trees. Unfortunately, they went in the wrong direction. They walked and walked, but there was no shelter anywhere.

"Let's try the next corner," pleaded Maya. But in that small alley only a wandering skinny cow and a mangy dog were to be seen.

The children were overwhelmed; they had never been in a big city. Shashi wanted to return to their own shelter, but they walked and walked and got further away and really lost. The dreadfully confused little children walked amidst the crowds of people, but no one looked at them, or cared that the lonely kids were in trouble.

All day they wandered around on the busy streets, in the hot, hot sun.

"Shashi, my big brother, I am so hungry," cried Maya, with tears rolling down her pale cheeks. Shashi usually carried a few coins in his pocket, but in his strange khaki

shorts, his pockets were empty. Not even one penny could he find. He couldn't buy a small roti and some dhal for his little sister.

They kept walking, desperately seeking their lost parents or at least a kind person who could help them. The people seemed to be busy and in a hurry and ignored them. Finally, they settled down in a small field overgrown with weeds and tall grass. They were too tired to talk and immediately fell asleep. Maya had a strange dream in which a soft voice whispered in her ear, "Take me home.....take me home". She woke up with tears in her eyes and found a small rock lying next to her head.

"Look Shashianna, I found a small rock," exclaimed Maya. "It is very pretty; imagine that, it even looks like a Ganesha! I was dreaming about it and it was telling me 'take me home, take me home'".

"Well maybe that little elephant god will bring us some good luck," remarked Shashi, "and soon we really might be able to go back home!"

Food from Heaven

*B*efore long, a woman and her six children arrived in the field. She ordered the children to stay there and to be good, then she left them. Maya looked curiously at the six children. They appeared to be hungry and scruffy with torn clothing and uncombed hair.

She went over to the biggest girl and asked, "What is your name? I am Maya, and my brother's name is Shashi. We are lost."

"I am Shanta and these are my brothers and sisters. Our mother has gone to buy us some food," answered the girl. "We do not have a home!"

Beside the dusty field stood a very tall, dirty- white building with a lot of windows and balconies. Suddenly a bundled up newspaper came flying out of one of the windows, plop, right in the middle of the children. Maya rushed to open it and she found that it contained some food!

Two Fried eggs, toast, an orange and an apple. The children gathered around and Shanta divided the fantastic breakfast equally amongst them.

"Food from Heaven", exclaimed Shashi surprised.

"What kind of building is that?" enquired Maya pointing to the towering wall.

"Oh, that is a hotel," answered Ramesh, one of the little boys.

"What is a hotel?" Shashi wanted to know.

"A hotel is like a shelter, but a large shelter, where people can stay for a short time when they are traveling," Shanta explained.

"Could my big brother and I stay there? We are looking for our Awwa, Appa and Adja," explained Maya. She thought that would be a brilliant idea!

"Ha, hah, they wouldn't let you in the door," snickered Pasha, another of the little boys who seemed to be the know- it- all type. "You need a lot of money to pay for a room."

Eventually the children's mother returned. She had a few rotis tied up in a cloth. Again they all gathered around in a circle and each one received a small piece of bread and a bit of dhal. Shashi and Maya were also given something to eat. After eating they all washed their faces and hands at the public water tap outside the field, and walked off down the street. Shashi held Maya's hand as they followed them.

"Listen boy and girl, if you want to eat you have to hold up this tin cup to all the people who pass by. They might give you a coin. You can keep that cup," the mother told Shashi and Maya.

"We had food from Heaven," piped up little Maya.

Grumbling the mother replied, "Food doesn't come from heaven, little girl."

"Amma, somebody threw a breakfast out of the window at the hotel, Maya thinks it came from heaven!" Pasha, the smart know–it-all boy, was happy to explain.

Maya was very sure and believed that the food wrapped in newspaper came down out of the sky. And that her little rock-Ganesha had indeed brought them some luck.

In the hotel was a family that had arrived from Canada the night before. While waiting for room service to bring them their breakfast the next morning, the three children walked out onto the balcony. They saw the group of youngsters down in the field. "Dad, what are those kids doing there?" the boy asked curiously. "Those are poor children, they have no home and have to beg for food," answered the Dad. "Come inside, your breakfast has arrived."

Hemant was a compassionate boy who had never encountered a homeless child. When his father mentioned that their breakfast had arrived, he decided he was not that hungry. He wrapped up his food in newspaper and threw it down from the balcony to the group of kids in the field.

And that is why Shashi thought the food was from Heaven

The Temple

The small group walked along for about a mile and reached an ancient temple. Shashi and Maya had never been to a temple.

"Maya, look a temple! Look at how beautiful it is with all the carvings, and there is a statue of Ganesha too."

They were in awe of the imposing building with towers and walls constructed from natural stone. The steps of the temple and the surroundings were very busy. Street vendors were trying to sell postcards, souvenirs, fruit and coconuts to the visitors. The mother and her six children sat down on the steps with other families who were hoping to receive alms from the devotees entering the temple.

Hand in hand Shashi and Maya climbed up the many steps leading to the dark, cool inner hall that housed Ganesha, the temple's main deity.

"We could say a prayer for our parents and Grandpa, Maya," said Shashi thoughtfully.

A strong fragrance of flowers mixed with incense filled the air.

A priest arrived and rang a bell. One of the devotees handed a coconut to the holy man, who cracked it open with a rock and gave everyone a small piece of the white fresh coconut and also a few drops of the coconut water. Then while reciting a religious song, he gave everyone a few loose flowers to throw over the god figure. A feeling of hope and peace filled the children's hearts.

They left the temple full of courage and decided to continue on the search for their parents and Grandpa. They said goodbye to the mother and her six children and walked away. When they passed by a public water tap, they used their tin cup to have a drink of cool water. All day long the children wandered along the busy streets. Cars were honking their horns; buses and trucks were winding in and out of traffic jams. The air was filled with noxious fumes, which made Maya cough frequently. She was pale and weak with hunger and slightly feverish .

The day drew to an end, and they still had no shelter and hadn't found their parents and grandfather. As the sun was setting, lamps were lit in the little shops on the roadsides. Evening was the best time for the vendors to sell their wares. People stopped at the stores for last minute supplies before heading home.

Shashi's stomach was rumbling, but he had no money to buy a simple meal for himself and his sister. They had not been very successful begging with their little tin cup. They were not used to asking strangers for charity. He felt so sad and lonely, and when he remembered the peaceful evenings at home in the village, he started to loose the courage to go on.

"How can I survive, find a job and a place to live?" he thought to himself.

Deep in thought he was not watching where he was going and bumped into a tall boy.

"Hey, watch where you are going kid," the boy snarled. He shook Shashi, and holding him by his shoulders he threw him to the ground and gave him a kick before moving on.

Shashi fell hard and hit his head on a rock. It started to bleed and he became unconscious.

"Shashi, Shashianna," cried Maya, "Somebody help us." But the people ignored her cry and just rushed on, minding their own business.

"I will go and get some water, Shashi and will be back quickly." She ran off with their tin cup to find a water tap.

The public water tap was around the corner, and when Maya came back to where she had left her brother, he wasn't there. She ran up and down the street, but couldn't find him. Maya looked around dumbfounded, she couldn't figure it out. Where had he gone? A piercing cry of sorrow escaped her. She slumped down on the hard ground and sobbed as if her heart was breaking.

Eventually she dried her tears with a tip of her long skirt. Across the busy street she noticed a fruit stand. Maybe someone from the store had noticed what had happened to her brother, thought Maya to herself. She decided to brave the traffic, and try to cross to the other side of the road. Miraculously, she made it unharmed.

"Please sir, I've lost my brother. Have you seen him?" she inquired of the friendly looking salesman.

"My dear little girl, what does your brother look like? Is he tall, is he small. Is he dark, is he fair?" inquired the man.

"Oh, his name is Shashi and he is about this tall," Maya showed him with her arm.

"My brother was pushed down and he bumped his head on a rock. I went to get him some water, and when I came back, he was gone," said Maya, looking up with big sad teary eyes.

"I did not notice anything happening on the other side of the road, but I have been very busy selling my lovely oranges. Here take one. They are so sweet right now," the vendor replied.

The kind man advised Maya to go back to the spot where she had lost the boy. He might come back looking for her.

Back under the large tree, Maya sat down on a rock, ate half of the orange and saved the rest for her brother. She waited a long, long time. Finally she dozed off, overcome by the heat, misery and sorrow. Suddenly, she felt a light tap on her shoulder. Looking up, she noticed a smart looking young woman in a sparkling clean white sari. The woman smiled sweetly and with empathy she inquired, "Why are you crying my little friend?"

Maya was trembling all over, and haltingly she related the long and weary story of the dreadful flood and their destroyed home.

"And now I can't find my brother, Shashi." She ended her narration sobbing.

"I think I know where he could be. I work at the new religious center close by. You told me that he was hurt, so maybe someone from the center took him in to take care of him. Let's go there anyway. You can stay there until we find your brother."

The woman lifted the distraught girl up and took hold of her hand. They did not have far to go. There in front of them stood an impressive building and at the door stood a watchman. The garden had an abundance of flowering bushes, and tall steps leading to large open doors.

Maya was really impressed. The watchman noticed the girl at once and said, "Are you the sister of the boy who was hurt? He was just asking for you and someone was ready to go and look for you."

The Sanctuary

"Oh yes, I am his sister," replied Maya very relieved. "Is my brother all right?"

"Go inside, someone will take you to him," suggested the watchman.

The kind lady took Maya inside. They entered the imposing cool marble hall.

A young boy also dressed in bright white clothes came to meet them, running down the stairway.

"Are you the little sister?" he asked. "Come with me I'll take you to him. He is going to be so relieved to see that you are safe."

The two children climbed the tall stairs, entered a room and there was Shashi resting on a narrow bed with a large bandage around his head. Maya ran to him and hugged him tenderly.

"Oh Shashianna, I was so scared when I couldn't find you!" Tears were streaming down her cheeks.

The nice lady entered the room with two plates of steaming rice and dhal.

"I expect you two are pretty hungry," she said. "There is a bathroom down the hall, you can freshen up there."

Food had never tasted so good; they ate every kernel of rice, and also licked the plates!

The lady spread out a bedroll for Maya, then tucked in the two lost and bedraggled kids, and wished them a good night.

Two days of rest and care were enough to heal Shashi's injuries. Maya was ready to continue on their search for their mother, father and grandfather. She passionately urged Shashi,

"Please big brother let's go now. We have to find our Awwa, Appa and Adja. I still have my Ganesha. I have a pocket in my skirt and kept him safe there. He will help us find Awwa Appa and Adja."

Shashi hesitated, because he thought his sister was safe now and they were being taken care of.

Shashi had already started to do small jobs for the staff in the large religious centre. But Maya was restless, she could not settle down, she insisted that their parents were somewhere out there in the city, and they had to go and find them. Finally, Shashi agreed. Quietly and unnoticed the two children left the sanctuary early one morning.

The Search Continues

*O*nce again they undertook the search for their family, walking in the awakening city on the busy streets and blending in with the rushing crowd. The tall buildings all around them made them feel so small and overwhelmed. They encountered a woman who was sweeping the street.

"Excuse me lady, could you direct us to the shelter where survivors of the flood are staying?" asked Maya.

"Dear children, I have no idea where that shelter could be. I am just a poor woman sweeping the streets for a few rupees a day."

And so the children moved on, walking, wandering, and asking anyone they met, "Have you seen our Awwa, Appa and Adja? Their names are Manju, Kollappa and Gangappa." The answer was usually, "Never heard of them, sorry."

Maya and Shashi learned to survive as homeless people living on the street. They begged, holding up the cup that was given to them by the woman with six children.

Sometimes they even had to steal some fruits from a fruit stand when the shopkeeper was looking the other way. Maya with her sweet face, large eyes and lovely long hair, could often get the attention of the ladies, and received the most coins in her cup.

As farm children, they were not used to too much luxury. They were tough kids, and always had to help their parents in the fields and with housekeeping chores. They had no running water in the home; they had to go to the well to fill the water containers. And Maya always had to help her mother wash clothes in the river.

Being alone without shelter or family and having nobody to talk to, was hard for the two lost youngsters to endure. They walked and wandered along the hot dusty roads and did their best to manage, all the while looking for Awwa, Appa and Adja. Then one day, they were caught in a sudden rainstorm. Luckily, they found shelter under a bridge with a group of other homeless families. A kind woman shared some of the meager food she had with the two hungry newcomers. Shashi once again related the story of their misery and how they were hoping to find their family.

Maya tried not to complain when in the morning she woke up with a splitting headache. She was shivery and sick in her stomach.

"Shashianna, I feel so bad today. I don't think I can come with you to search for our lost family. I will just stay here and sleep a bit longer," she whimpered in a small voice.

Shashi was very concerned, he felt Maya's hands and forehead, she was extremely hot.

"Oh Maya, little sister. You are very sick, I have to take you to the hospital," he said with much concern.

He let her climb up on his back and started walking. But where, oh where was the hospital?

There at the corner of a busy intersection stood a police officer.

"Maya you sit here on this rock, while I ask the policeman where I can find a hospital, or a doctor's clinic."

"Sir," Shashi asked politely, "my little sister is very sick, she has a high fever. I want to take her to the nearest clinic or hospital. Could you direct me please?"

"Yes, sure, there is one not far from here. Just follow this road to the next stop, and turn left. You'll see a white building on your right. That is the clinic," directed the police officer.

"But where are your parents?" he asked. "You should go home."

"Kind sir, we can't find our parents. They were lost during the flood in our village. We have been looking for them for many days already."

"All right now go to the clinic. They will look after your sister, and also help you find your parents."

"Come on Maya, I know where it is. Can you walk a bit now?" Maya tried to stand up, but collapsed into her brother's arms.

"I'll carry you, climb on my back again. The policeman told me the clinic is not far from here."

At The Medical Clinic

*T*he clinic was very busy; people were sitting in rows on benches and on the floor.

Shashi rushed in sweating and out of breath, carrying Maya in his arms.

"Please take care of my sister, she has a very high fever," he cried out sorrowfully.

A nurse looked at the children. She came over to them and felt Maya's forehead and hands.

"Yes, she has a fever, but you will still have to wait a while. There are many sick people already waiting for their turn. Sit down over there, and I will call you soon."

She brought a cold wet cloth to put on Maya's forehead, and gave them both some water to drink.

The children waited patiently for a long, long time. Finally, the doctor was able to attend to them.

"Your sister needs to go to the hospital. She is very sick. You must call your parents to come and get her," the doctor told them with a stern voice.

"Doctor, Sir, we have no parents. We couldn't find them when we were rescued from the flood," Shashi told him, desperately trying to control his tears.

"I am sorry about your misfortune, but what am I to do?" said Doctor Anand, scratching his head. He called the social worker who was still in the clinic.

"Hey Shekhar, come here. These children need a ride to the hospital. Could you take them?"

Shekhar kindly agreed and they carried Maya to his van.

The Hospital

Maya was immediately admitted on arrival. The nurse removed most of her clothes and put her in a lukewarm bath to cool down the high fever. She then dressed her in a hospital gown, and started an IV with prescribed medication. Shahsi was allowed to sit at her bedside. The doctor came by in the evening and checked her temperature and felt her pulse. He looked very seriously at Shahsi, shook his head and said, "I am afraid your sister is very sick. She might have meningitis, a very serious disease. You should make every effort to find your family. Somebody should be here with you."

Once again poor Shashi had to tell his sad story.

"Who brought you here Shashi, was he a relative?"

"No Sir," answered the boy, "that was Shekhar a social worker from the clinic."

"I'll contact him. He could take you to the Red Cross office, you may be able to identify your parents there. They have lists of survivors from the flood disaster."

Maya was unconscious, moaning a little, and moving her arms and legs.

Shashi took her hand, stroked it softly and whispered, "My little sister, don't worry. You are going to be all right. I can take care of you, I am old enough. I can find a job or we can go back to the Sanctuary. You can go to school and I can work there."

Tears were running down the young boy's sorrowful face.

Then he found the little rock Ganesha in his sister's pocket. He laid it down next to Maya's hand.

"Dear Ganesha, please take care of my sister," he whispered.

Shashi stayed with Maya throughout the night. He slept on a towel on the floor next to her bed.

Early the next morning Shekhar came in. They stood quietly observing the sleeping Maya. She seemed to be less restless.

"Your sister looks a bit better, Shahsi, she is going to be all right," he reassured the weary boy.

"Let's go and have some breakfast and then we'll go to the Red Cross office."

Shekhar's heart was aching for the two unfortunate children.

He was a very kind man, a man with a small family of his own. He could empathize with the children, who must be anxious and terrified to be lost and lonely in the big city,

The Red Cross Office

Hesitatingly, Shashi entered the Red Cross office building, hiding behind the strong back of Shekhar. They waited silently in line for their turn at the counter. It was a very busy day at the Red Cross office. Shashi was impressed with how efficiently the staff worked, listening to the complaints and stories of the people, and offering assistance whenever possible.

Finally, it was Shashi's turn. Suddenly he was speechless, shaking with anxiety, and stared at the agent with big teary eyes. Shekhar stood beside him and put a steadying hand on his shoulder.

"This young man has lost home and family in the recent floods in his village. He would like to go through a list of survivors, if you please."

"My name is Shobha. I will give you a list, but first I have to know your name, your father's and mother's names. I also need to know the name of your village and district."

Shashi dried his tears and with a trembling voice gave the information to Shobha:

"My father's name is Kollappa, my mother is called Manju, and our last name is Patil.

And my name is Shashi. My sister Maya is in the hospital. My Grandfather who lived with us is also lost. His name is Gangappa Goudar. Our village was Shivapuru, in the district of Shigoan."

"You are a clever boy. With that information we might be able to help you. Let's find the correct list. Come with me to the back office. There you can take your time and look up your parents and Grandpa."

The young boy followed Shobha to a back room with a desk and chairs. A large box with files was put in front of them.

Shekhar took out the first list of names of friends and village members who were miraculously saved, and prayed the names of the boy's family members would be amongst them.

Shashi began to turn pages, checked names, addresses, again and again, but did not find the names of his father or mother. But one name caught his eye.

"Could that be Grandfather?" he asked Shobha who had just come in.

They made sure name and address were correct. It could very well be Grandfather Goudar.

"Does this mean he is alive?" the distraught boy asked with a trembling voice.

Shobha entered the name in her computer and waited.

"Look here Shashi, it is your grandfather, and he is alive. He is in Shivapuru helping with the cleanup. I will immediately send a message to him that you and your sister are here in the city."

"Maya is very sick but I am sure this good news will speed up her recovery," said Shashi. He was so excited. At the same time he realized sorrowfully that he had not found his Awwa and Appa yet.

Little Maya

While Shashi was at the Red Cross Office, Maya woke up and she felt much better. The IV had been removed; her temperature was back to normal, her headache was also gone. There on the bed she found her Ganesha again. She hopped out of bed and started calling for her brother.

"Shashi I feel much better, we can go now." But her brother wasn't there. She found her clothes, got dressed and skipped out of the room. With bare feet, the little girl skipped along the long deserted hallway until she reached the exit. There she sat down on the front steps and decided to wait for the return of her brother.

A little off-white puppy shared the front steps with the little girl.

"Hey there puppy, are you lost?" asked Maya curiously.

The little puppy looked at her with large pleading eyes and wagged its tail at Maya. Then it jumped into her lap. Tenderly Maya embraced the little doggy.

"Do you want to stay with me? My big brother will say, 'We can't take care of a dog. We can hardly take care of ourselves!' But I will never let you go, you'll see."

She stroked the doggy, rubbed its tummy and announced, "Your name will be Surya, which means sun."

And that was how Shashi found her. He came along waving both arms in the air and shouting excitedly, "Maya, Maya, I have good news. Adja is alive! He is in Shivapuru helping with the cleanup of the town. But why are you outside?"

"I am fine now. I came looking for you. Did you say Adja is all right and in our village? What about Awwa and Appa, are they also in Shivapuru with Grandfather?" asked Maya, holding the dog tightly in her arms.

"Dear little sister, I did not find our parents names on the lists, but we will keep looking. Now the first thing is for you to get much better so that we can travel to our village and meet Adja. A truck with drinking water is leaving from the Red Cross Office in a few days. They offered to take us to Shivapuru. I came to see if you were better and if you would be able to make the trip in the next few days. It is good to see you are feeling better."

"Shashianna, I am taking this puppy with me. I promised it that I would take care of it, and I will." Shashi did not have the heart to refuse her.

A few days later when the doctor said it was okay for Maya to travel, the two children and the dog walked back to the Red Cross Office, and were just in time to get a ride to their village.

Returning to the Disaster Area

After a long journey, the truck carrying large bottles of drinking water, stopped at the temporary emergency building in Shivapuru. Shashi and Maya got down from the truck. They could see destroyed homes, rice fields covered with dried up mud, and destroyed terraces. This was a very disturbing sight for the two young children.

"Where was our home Shashi?" asked Maya anxiously.

"Let's go up the hill and find Adja." Shashi took Maya's hand and they walked slowly up the hill to the desolate ruins of their village.

A group of volunteers was busy salvaging lumber and household items from the flattened homes. An old man was bent over a pile of weathered boards, with a narrow unshaven face, a torn shirt and muddy pants. He turned around surprised when he heard someone calling, "Adja, is that you?" To his tremendous joy he recognized his two grandchildren approaching him.

48

"Oh, my dear children, how grateful I am to see you," he exclaimed.

He embraced them tightly. Maya and Shashi clung to their grandfather as if they could never let go!

The dear old man was overcome with emotion. "You are alive, it is a miracle. I did get a message from the Red Cross office, but could not believe it."

Sadly, Shashi had to tell Adja that they had not been successful in finding their parents yet. The reunion of these three people was a token of hope for a better future.

"Adja, we want to help you. Tell us what we can do," offered Shashi spontaneously.

"You two can certainly help, as there is much work to be done here. You can help to sort out the rubble into a pile of items to be saved and another pile for items to be burned up later.

The children started sorting through the rubble.

In the evening all the volunteers gathered around the open fire, had dinner and related their experiences during the disaster, and how they were able to survive. Maya showed them her little Ganesha rock statue, and told everybody how she found it, and that it had brought them luck in helping them find their grandfather.

Many days were spent working hard in the hot sun. Slowly some order was restored and plans could now be made for rebuilding. Maya's little puppy, Surya, ran around all day and was loved by everyone, and spoiled with bits of food.

One evening, Grandfather decided to discuss the children's future with them. Maya was anxious to start school.

"I will study hard to learn about floods, so that I can make sure we will never have them anymore," she announced.

Shashi was more reluctant to go back to school and leave his grandfather. He liked village life and working on the land. Also, city life scared him, especially after his experience of being homeless on the streets. Maya would attend the primary school in the village, but Shashi would have to go to school in another town, and he would have to live at the school during the school year. Grandfather had no money, as he had lost everything in the flood. He wondered how he would pay for Shashi's education.

"Shashi we do not have to decide right now. We will continue the work here; repair the homes and the rice paddies and sow new seeds. A solution will eventually be found," was Grandfather's wise comment.

The Messenger

*O*ne day as they were working to rebuild the village, Maya called out, "Adja, look! There comes our friend Shekhar" She was delighted to see Shekhar and ran to him and hugged him tightly.

"Namaskara Adjare, how are you?" Shekhar greeted Grandfather politely.

"We are doing very well, friend. The children are great workers and fortunately we have managed to get some order into this horrifying disaster area. We are developing plans to rebuild the village and replant the rice fields," answered Grandfather proudly.

"I am pleased to see that you all are doing so well, but I have come to give you some very sad news," announced Shekhar with a very serious expression on his face. "Let's sit down somewhere where we can talk quietly." They sat down under a lonely shady tree.

"I am very sorry to have to tell you Shashi and Maya, we found out that your Mother and Father died in the flood."

This was a shock for the three survivors. Maya wept softly, while Shashi stared off in the distance to where once their home stood. He put his arms around his sister. Grandfather covered his face with both hands, tears steaming down his thin lined cheeks. Surya, the little puppy may have realized that something was wrong. He snuggled up to Maya and put his head in her lap. Maya had steadfastly believed that they would find Awwa and Appa eventually. Shashi and Adja on the other hand, had almost given up hope of finding them alive. All the same it was painful news for them to hear.

"We have organized a service to remember all the villagers and your family members who were lost in the flood. We will hold the memorial here on Sunday. There will be a priest and musicians and all the volunteers will join us too."

The three sad people stayed together quietly, talking quietly and remembering the dear family members they had lost.

A Promise of Courage

Where oh where are all the people
The cows, the goats, the dogs and cats
The grains we harvested, the fields, our homes

It's almost impossible to comprehend
The magnitude of the destruction
Where once there was a peaceful village
Nothing is left but mud and ruins

But we who have survived, we will overcome
We will salvage, dig and clean
Repair the dikes, plant new seeds

Against tremendous odds we will strive
To rebuild the homes, the fields
We've returned to bring new life
Undertake with courage
The enormous task
That is our promise.

On Sunday the villagers and volunteers gathered together to remember the people they had lost in the flood. The priest chanted a prayer and musicians played melodious music. Everyone enjoyed the soothing sound and joined to recite the song of courage.

Shekhar had praise for all the work already accomplished and he had encouraging words for everyone to go on and make every day count.

Shashi told Maya and Grandfather, "Don't worry Adja, I will always look after you and my little sister."

A beautiful sunset filled the sky with bright colors, a promise of hope and courage.

Information about growing rice in India

Facts: 2/3 rd of the world population is dependent on rice as a staple food.

In India alone 70-80% of the population eat rice with every meal.

Rice needs to grow submerged in water.

But there are some kinds if rice that can grow on dry land too.

Rice or Paddy fields are mostly irrigated by a large reservoir lake, a river or rainfall.

Some fields are built up on a hill or mountainside with little dykes and run offs.

Seedlings are planted manually in the wet soil.

The plants are very green until the rice ripens and turns brown. Then usually in villages the rice stalks are cut, also manually, with a scythe, then threshed in the fields and the kernels collected in bags or baskets.

The winnowing is separating kernels from the chaff, by shaking the hulls on a flat tray like basket, in the wind so that the chaff can fly away, and leave the kernels clean and dry. This is also usually done in the fields.

It is believed that rice plants were discovered in India, growing in the wild and then cultivated in about 5000-3000 BC.

Rice plants in India need moist and warmth. A subtropical climate is preferred.

India, China and Indonesia are the leading rice producing nations in the world.

The rice plant

The rice plant belongs to the grain growing grass family.

Depending on the climate the rice plant has a life span of about 3 to 7 months.

Some regions in India have two harvests per year.

Rice is not a water plant, but needs a large amount of water for the planting and growing.

The rice crops are very dependent on the weather. Drought or too much rain can destroy the plant.

The rice plant is ready for harvesting when the husks turn brown, and is now called paddy. The fields are drained dry before the harvesting.

One paddy is a complete seed of rice. Each paddy has many layers,

The first layer is called the husk. Then comes the next layer, called bran.

The bran is the most nutritious part of the rice grain.

The inner part is the kernel this consists of starch and the embryo, which can grow into a new plant.

Information from: All about rice in India.
www.fao.org.rice2004/en/p6.htm.
And from: Rice Trade:
www.rice-trade.com/threshing.html

About the Author

*W*obine Ishwaran started writing for children after retirement. Born in the Netherlands, she lived as a child with her family for several years in South Africa, Indonesia and in the Netherlands. During her studies to become a registered nurse, she met her husband, K. Ishwaran, a PhD student from India. They married in India, had two children and then immigrated to Canada, where their third son was born.

Wobine lives in Toronto and has published with Author House in the U.S, and Trafford Publishing in Vancouver. She loves to read, write and has traveled several times to India. This story, about the two courageous children, is very close to her heart.

Also by Wobine Ishwaran:

Spunky Sprout in India

The fly Away Kite
A Toronto island picnic

A Journey into Space
Kary to the Moon

Published by Author House US

Kiki's Adventures

The Disappearing Toys

Ricky and Silver Splash
A Story About a Boy and his fish

Published by Trafford Publishing
Victoria, Canada